Little, Brown Presents:
The Nuts
Keep Rolling!
by Eric Litwin
illustrated by
Scott Magoon
LB
Little, Brown and Company
New York Boston

Hazel and Wally were really small.
They wanted to be big and tall.

PAT, PAT

PAT,
PAT

So they rolled through sticky
mud and goo.
The more they rolled,
the bigger they grew.

And they sang this song.

KEEP ROLLING.
KEEP ROLLING.
KEEP ROLLING.

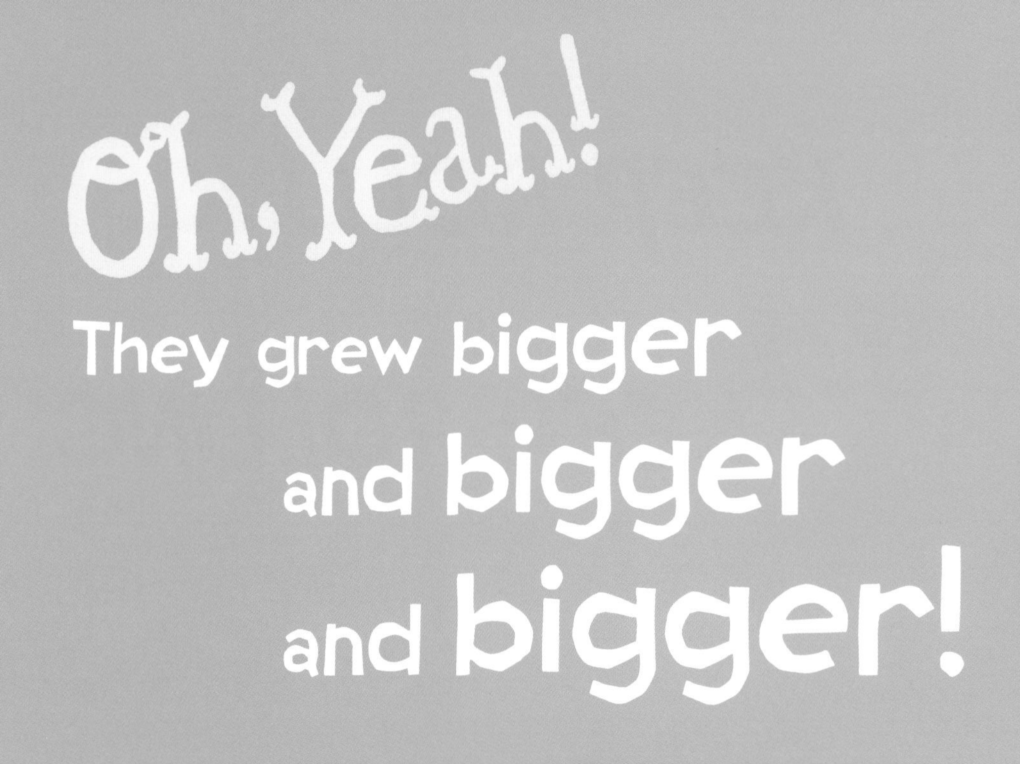

Oh, Yeah!

They grew bigger
and bigger
and bigger!

Now they were the size of cats.
Hazel and Wally were smiling until...

...a pack of dogs
came over the hill.
Oh, No!
What can they do?
KEEP ROLLING!
Grr!
Bark!
RUFF!

KEEP ROLLING.
KEEP ROLLING.
KEEP ROLLING.
Arf!
DOGWOOD FOREST

They grew bigger
and **bigger**
and **bigger!**

Now they were the size of big dogs.
Hazel and Wally were giggling until...

...the dogcatcher came over the hill.

Oh, No!

What can they do?

KEEP ROLLING!

KEEP ROLLING.
KEEP ROLLING.
KEEP ROLLING.

Oh, Yeah!

They grew bigger

and bigger

and bigger!

Now they were the size of...

...ELEPHANTS!

Hazel and Wally were
laughing until...

...the zookeeper came over the hill.

Oh, No!

What can they do?

KEEP ROLLING!

ZOO

KEEP ROLLING.

KEEP ROLLING.

KEEP ROLLING.

Oh, No!

It started to rain.
The sky turned gray.
The mud and the goo
were all washed away.

And they became smaller

and smaller

and smaller!

Now they were little
and out there alone.
But Hazel and Wally
knew how to get home.

What can they do?

KEEP ROLLING.

KEEP ROLLING.
KEEP ROLLING.
KEEP ROLLING.

Oh, Yeah!

They rolled to their house.
It was cozy and bright.
Mama and Papa Nut
hugged them so tight.

And that family was happy,
even though they were small.
Because when you have each other,
then you have it all.

the end

Download the KEEP ROLLING song and dance at TheNutFamily.com!

To my dear friend Susan and Mr. B the Zen doggie. —EL

For Tommy F...keep rolling! —SM

About This Book

This book was edited by Allison Moore and designed by Kristina Iulo with art direction from Saho Fujii; the production was supervised by Erika Schwartz, and the production editor was Annie McDonnell. The digital illustrations were created using Adobe Photoshop and a very nutty imagination. The book was printed on 128gsm Gold Sun matte paper. The text and display type were set in Skizzors, and the jacket was hand-lettered by the illustrator.

Little, Brown and Company

Hachette Book Group
1290 Avenue of the Americas, New York, NY 10104
Visit us at lb-kids.com

Little, Brown and Company is a division of Hachette Book Group, Inc.
The Little, Brown name and logo are trademarks of Hachette Book Group, Inc.

The publisher is not responsible for websites (or their content) that are not owned by the publisher.

First Edition: April 2017

ISBN 978-0-316-32251-5

10 9 8 7 6 5 4 3
APS
PRINTED IN CHINA